Kid Games, Lessons Learned

Chip Kroll

Acknowledgments

My influence for this book comes from several inspirations: Robert Fulghum, my favorite author, with his animated, easy to enjoy short-story style; Craig Shoemaker and his comedy routines of life as a child; and of course, the movie *A Christmas Story* as directed by Bob Clark. In addition, Richard Simmons for his dedication to child exercise and fight against obesity.

I would like to thank Amy, Jill, Susan, Rick, and Jacque for sharing their experiences playing childhood games and adding depth to the stories. And especially Dennis, for giving consultation as a veteran of the Vietnam War and serving our country.

My sincere appreciation goes to my editor, Sandra. She corrected my grammar better than any of my English professors and added the right amount of polish to the rough spots.

Of course, my mom and dad deserve the dedication of this book for loving, guiding, and raising me to succeed and learn the lessons of life.

Mom, all these tales are fictitious and never happened to me. Right, Dad?

Contents

Chapter 1 – Let the Games Begin

The time is present day. Susie and Pete are enjoying the Christmas tradition back at home with their parents and their own families, except their older brother is missing. Russell is spending the season away with his wife's family. This brings back the anxiety of the 1969 holidays when he served in Vietnam. Reminisce with Pete in the warm family kitchen as he recalls the games he and Susie played as kids, and the lessons they learned.

The afternoon was chilly at the family homestead following a delightful Christmas lunch. The living room felt warm from the fireplace while the tree twinkled. Mom snuggled up reading her new book, Dad dozed on the couch with the paper, and our better halves enjoyed the excitement of the children playing with their new toys from Santa. He had fulfilled their wishes.

Susie and I were cleaning up in the kitchen as we always did together. As I sat down for my afternoon coffee watching my fraternal twin sister finish, I became overwhelmed, recalling the fond memories of our childhood. I seldom see my sister these days. We live a far distance apart from each other and are both busy raising our own families. However, we share a soul, and Christmas is always our special time.

Susie came into the world a full five minutes after me, yet everyone knew me as Susie's brother. No one ever called her Pete's sister. Her infectious giggle made my sister unique. Susie was Susie. She was popular, cute, outrageous, and constantly getting us into trouble. My role as her partner in crime was to stay calm, collected, and constantly get us out of trouble. The great adventures we experienced, the eternal bond we formed, and the lessons we learned growing up together were worth the effort.

This year found both of us dearly missing our older brother Russell. We knew he was safe, celebrating Christmas with his wife's family on the other side of the country. However, his absence always brings back the memory of when he was serving in Vietnam and missing from the family Christmas table in 1969. Susie and I were fifth graders, on the verge of adulthood.

And scared.

Susie finished and sat down next to me in the warmth of our family kitchen. I began to reminisce and said, "Do you remember the time…"

Before another word came out, she gently said, "Of course, Pete. I always remember the time spent with you."

The year was 1969. Neil Armstrong walked on the moon, the war was raging in Vietnam, the hippies were making love, and Susie and Pete were fraternal twins growing up. They were fifth graders on the verge of adulthood, playing youthful games together and forming an inseparable bond.

Chapter 2 – Marco Has Left the Building

Susie and I enjoyed riding our bikes to the pool throughout the summer, especially jumping into the cool water during the hottest part of the day. All our friends were usually there, and we had fun racing everybody or playing games like Sharks and Minnows.

One day Dad left early from his work and came home wanting to go swimming before dinner. Of course, my sister and I always accepted an offer for a ride to the pool in the car. Mom and Dad often brought us on the weekend, as did other families to spend the day with their children. When we were younger, Dad would stand in the deep part of the water while we took turns swimming out to him. He would hold us for a moment to catch our breath, then push us back toward the edge so the next one could dive in. Our dad always held us safely in his arms, which gave a warm feeling of protection and love.

Susie and I watched our mom and dad gently swim laps and enjoy their moment relaxing together. That made both of us very happy. They were no longer concerned about us being at the pool or keeping a watchful eye. However, we all worried about our older brother, Russell, serving in Vietnam. None of us could truly relax until he safely returned home to be with us once again.

Spending time at the pool as a family briefly released the tension and offered a small amount of relief.

The pool began to empty in the cool part of the day as Susie and I were playing the game Marco Polo. Dad stood up and without saying a word, swung his arm, motioning to the entire pool that it was time to leave. Of course, only mom started gathering up our belongings. My sister kept her eyes tightly closed, calling out "Marco" as I yelled "Polo" while heading to the edge of the pool to leave. The lifeguard came down from his chair after watching us play. As I climbed out of the pool, he stood over me at the ladder. Susie yelled out another loud "Marco" as she continued to play the game, not knowing Dad had summoned us to go. Before I could tell my sister the game was over, the lifeguard yelled "Polo" in a voice that could have been my own! Susie appeared slightly confused and replied "Marco?" She thought there might be water in her ears. Mom enjoyed watching the spectacle of Susie remaining completely oblivious to this novel development in our game as she held our belongings. Dad was already at the men's shower room entrance and waving his arm for me to hurry. The game continued as the skillful hunter rapidly closed in on her prey, and everybody at the pool was now watching with interest. As she neared the ladder, the lifeguard sharply blew his whistle and shouted in an authoritative voice, "Stop playing games now!" Susie quickly opened her eyes and looked baffled not seeing me. She saw the lifeguard smiling and suddenly realized he had been Polo! Everybody at the pool laughed. Mom smiled and called her to come on, Dad was waiting to leave. The show had been quite humorous. Susie appreciated the trick played on her and started giggling. Since my sister could always laugh at herself, she always stayed happy and amused. Her infectious giggle meant she was especially delighted.

Chapter 3 – Flapper Tape Parade

Our older brother Russell had been a construction worker before signing up to become a Seabee in the Navy. He was a natural and already had the "Can Do" attitude.

On his way to Vietnam, he bought a low-cost tape recorder, then sent the family recordings of his voice telling us his adventures in addition to pictures and letters. Mom announced a package had arrived from Russell as Susie and I came in the back door from playing at the park all day. We were always excited to hear our brother's voice on the modern transistor reel-to-reel tape player that Dad bought, although, the tubes still needed to warm up in the stereo while the family ate supper.

Afterward, everyone eagerly watched dad put the tape on the player, turn the volume up, and we squealed with excitement when the tape began moving. Russell always started by talking to Mom and Dad, assuring the family he was fine and how much he missed and loved us all.

Tonight, he told us a story about meeting a tough Marine named Jack in the mess hall. He noticed Jack holding a photo in his hand before eating, so Russell decided to sit across from him and asked, "Who are you thinking about?" The Marine replied that he was missing his twin sister at home. She always got him out of the trouble he was always getting into. Russell said he told Jack he understood. "I have younger twin siblings at home. Susie is always getting them into trouble and Pete is always getting them out." With that, my sister wrinkled her nose defiantly and then giggled. She knew that was true.

He continued, "Jack showed me the worn laminate photo of his sister, and written on the back was 'Wish I were there to keep my eye on you, Love Sis.'" Russell finished the story by telling us, "His sister is as pretty as Susie. I hope to stay in touch with Jack after we get home."

We decided the next day to team up on decorating our bikes to honor Russell and his Seabee friends in the upcoming Fourth of July parade in the park. Dad showed us how to create a replica of his battalion by using the photograph he sent. We transposed dots from the image to the large placard, connected them, then colored with crayons to construct a bigger than life picture. I taped the large poster on my bike with flags; Susie put a sign on her bike that said, "Our brother and his friends keep us safe." Susie and I even stuck flappers on to make lots of noise with the spokes. We finished by covering our bikes with red, white, and blue crepe paper to show our American pride.

On the Fourth of July, we rang our bells, honked our horns, and waved at everybody with big smiles as we rode our bikes in the parade. Susie and I were very proud of our brother and his friends for serving our country. We must have looked good because our picture appeared in the town paper the next day. Mom bought several copies and sent our picture to Russell, along with our letters of love.

A few months later, a package sent directly to Susie and myself arrived from Russell. It sat unopened and waiting on the dining room table as we came in. This seemed unusual: he normally sent mail addressed to the family, and Mom opened his parcels by tradition. Susie and I anxiously opened the box. We found dozens of envelopes addressed to us from everybody in the picture we drew, including our brother's commander. Every letter said thank you for remembering them. They enjoyed Russell sharing his crazy messages from Susie and appreciated my wonderful job taking care of my sister and our family.

I noticed the Seabees likely experienced bad weather, because several of the letters seemed smeared by raindrops. Susie quietly said, "They might be tears."

Chapter 4 – Teetering on the Edge

Susie and I often rode our bikes to the community park. A big reason was to see the ice cream man; he always drove by and summoned us with his magic bell. We saved part of our weekly allowance for ice-cold ice cream every trip. Today was hot and humid, just after the Fourth of July, a perfect day to play in the shade of the trees. The holiday gave the park vibrant, new splendor. Bright red, white, and blue enamel paint brought the three teeter-totters (or seesaws, as our cousins called them) to patriotic life. Susie wore her new red shorts and wanted to ride the matching one. My sister was great at inventing different games to make the time fun. We went up and down at least a million times!

Suddenly, the magic call of the ice cream bell for our ice-cold afternoon treat sounded. We always raced each other to be the first one at the ice cream truck. I instantly jumped off and ran as fast as I could, not waiting for Susie.

I arrived at the ice cream truck shouting, "I win!" while the ice cream man was waiting. He looked confused and asked, "I see you easily won today, where's your little sister?" He always teased Susie by calling her "my little sister," knowing that I was a full five minutes older than her. Now I felt confused and concerned that Susie was not with me. The ice cream man noticed my panicked look as I fumbled for the money to pay him. He handed me our favorite treat that we always bought and said, "Go find your little sister; I'm sure she's fine. It's a humid day and I know you two enjoy those seesaws. Wouldn't surprise me one bit if you find her stuck to one like a fly on a frog's tongue. Happens to kids all the time after the city painted them for the Fourth of July." I thanked him and quickly went running back to the teeter-totters with our ice cream treats to find out what happened to Susie.

When I returned, Susie was stuck to the red teeter-totter and mad as an angry hornet, exactly as the ice cream man predicted. Her matching red shorts glued her forever to the red teeter-totter. She was upset with me for leaving her behind after she shouted at me to wait. The race had started and I did not hear my sister's call for help. Susie always admitted that she depends on me to get her out of trouble.

After thinking for a moment on how to free Susie from the eternal grasp of the playground equipment, I instructed her to roll her bottom back and forth on the enamel painted wood and gently pull on her shorts to give a little extra oomph. She finally came loose and slid off the edge. Free at last!

What my sister did not see were the two orange push-ups in my hands. Her favorite! I told Susie I was sorry, but we needed to have our ice cream. That's when she noticed the ice cream treat I had brought for her. Susie almost knocked the push-ups out of my hand giving me a big hug! That was the best ice cream we ever enjoyed together. Susie started a new tradition and buys my ice cream at the park, even to this day!

Chapter 5 – I Shot an Arrow into the Air

Susie played a small part in the school play this year. She did not speak a single word. Her character stood on stage and appeared completely innocent with a broken lamp that she obviously had broken. The parents carried the dialog by arguing about how the destruction of their fragile antique had occurred. Only thing missing was an angelic halo over her head; she had the perfect smile and facial expressions. The audience could not believe she was guilty, even after seeing her throw the prop down and smashing it into a million pieces. My sister thought that was the best part. She received applause from the audience for her acting ability. Susie the drama queen was born.

The neighborhood kids occasionally played cowboys & Indians. This simple game did not require much skill, so the players were all equal. Moreover, we didn't care who won or lost; lying in the shade on the cool grass felt especially comfortable on hot days. We only needed our imagination to recreate the Wild West, using our fingers for guns and pretending to have bows and arrows.

Cowboys and Indians was not high on the list of Susie's favorite games, not sports-oriented enough for her. She only liked to play dead next to me so we could talk. We would look at the clouds and enjoy chatting the rest of the game until one side would finally win. Although, I preferred having my sister on my side. She would cover my back and I usually lived longer.

However, Susie was a savage on the opposing team. Didn't matter where she started at the beginning. My sister would run directly at me to attack, out in the open at the start of every game. Moreover, when I'd shoot her before she could get close, she'd fall down and roll all the way across the battlefield to play dead right under my feet, then quickly get me eliminated by distracting me. I usually didn't mind missing most of the action conversing with my sister.

In today's skirmish, Susie played a cowboy and I was an Indian. She came over before the game started and told me to shoot her with an arrow. Why did my sister say this? I always shot her. She obviously wanted to tell me something important. At the appointed time, she came charging out into the open from behind the fence and ran straight at me. I sprang up, let go an imaginary arrow, and shouted, "Got you, Susie, you're dead!" Unexpectedly, she pulled a small tree limb from out of nowhere and stuck it under her arm. Holy Gun Smoke! I shot her with a real arrow! My sister acted dramatically while swirling and staggering around better than any cartoon. She finally collapsed in the grass under a tree. Whoomp! All the boys were under Susie's control, watching her every move. Nobody had seen anything like that before.

Suddenly all the Indians suffered massive heart attacks! The Indians ran out, clutched their chest, and dropped like flies in the middle of the playground. The cowboys wiped out the entire tribe without firing a single shot. Game over! The Indians were now excited to be cowboys and be struck in the heart with real arrows. We jumped up and ran to the nearest trees looking for the right-size limbs. Every tree in the neighborhood stood bare that summer from the ground up to as high as we could reach.

My sister captured the attention of every boy on the playground that day. We thought Susie was one of us. Except she wasn't anymore; she was becoming a woman and cast a magic spell. We were learning the facts of life.

Chapter 6 – Outta the Park!

Susie was a star at tennis, and I am much better shooting marbles. About the only game we both have equal skill playing is whiffle ball. One morning after breakfast, my sister and I decided to play a two-player game and determine the best whiffle ball player. The field was our front yard. We agreed you were out if the fielder caught the ball in the air or rolling on the ground, and two foul balls count as an out. The batter needed to hit the ball past the pitcher mound, blah, blah, blah on rules. Whoever led after nine innings would be the champion. After the ceremonious flip of a coin, Susie chose to be the home team, and I batted first.

We found the score tied at the end of regulation play. Both teams were tired and our game went into extra innings. The rules stated that the champion would be whoever was ahead at the end of the inning.

Susie and I played all morning concluding each inning in a tie with no end in sight. Mom finally called us in for lunch, and we enjoyed the break. The game started again after lunch. We played hard all afternoon; nobody could win! Several kids stopped and asked if they could play. My sister told them, "No, this is a game between only Pete and me to find out who the champion is!"

It was nearly dark; my sister and I played for hours and knew mom was going to call us in to have supper soon. Susie came to bat while I was ahead by a single run. She began to tire and tried to whack the ball hard, but popped the first two up for easy outs. Her third swing hit the ball on the ground for a routine play. However, I did not want to beat my sister with an easy out. When the ball came to me, I kicked the ball all the way to the home run zone and tied the game again. Susie had no idea why, but this ignited her last ounce of adrenaline. The next turn she smacked the ball and sent it sailing high over my head. My sister certainly won the game with her perseverance. I turned to run after the ball with little enthusiasm. As luck would have it, the ball hit on the sidewalk and continued to roll. With the last of my energy, I caught up and grabbed the rolling ball. Susie was out and tied the game again! We competed for the championship all day long and were beyond exhaustion. The sun had set and the stadium was dark. Were we going to play another inning?

Mom came out on the porch and watched the last play. She announced, "The game is over. I have never seen you two this intense playing together. You've been at this all day long. Time to come in and eat supper!" With that, she went back inside.

As I ran back carrying the ball, Susie was waiting with the bat. Susie asked, "Why didn't you beat me when you had the chance?" I responded, "I didn't want to be the champion on an easy play." Then I asked, "Why did you hit the ball on the sidewalk and let me get you out?" She denied any such doing. "You made a hard play to get me out! That ball went where it wanted!" I knew better, that ball went exactly where Susie wanted.

In my official-sounding voice I said, "I declare my sister, Susie, and I are both champions at whiffle ball and should never play each other again to see who's the best!" Susie gave me a big hug and softly said, "Why did you say that? You're always a champion to me!" And she always made me feel like one.

Chapter 7 – Heidi and Go Seek

The house next door had been for sale, and Susie and I finally spotted SOLD on the sign. We wondered who bought the house. The next week, a large moving van pulled up in the morning, and we noticed the family had a girl who appeared to be our age. That afternoon, Susie and I walked over to introduce ourselves and meet the new neighbors. We knocked on the door and a man answered. I said, "Hi, I'm Pete and this is my sister Susie. We live next door and wondered if the girl we saw could come out and play?" The man smiled and with a heavy accent introduced himself. He explained they were from Germany and he was starting a new job here. He called out "Heidi" over his shoulder and turned back to us. He continued, telling us that Heidi did not speak English and may not understand what we said. I told him, "That's ok, nobody understands Susie anyway." With that, Susie smacked me and said, "Everybody understands me, and I'll bet even Heidi does." Heidi came to the door and looked at us, maybe a little scared. Susie made the first move, pointed at herself, and said, "I'm Susie." She smiled big and with her infectious giggle, gave Heidi a hug, took her hand and pulled her out to play. As Heidi was being dragged away, she was smiling as big as Susie and giggling too. Those two became instant pals.

Heidi's father looked at me, chuckling, and said, "I don't understand Susie, yet I understand Susie. You have a special sister." Oh boy, that was an understatement. I let him know we wouldn't be far, just to yell for Heidi like all the other parents when he wanted her to come home.

In only a week, Susie was speaking German as fast as Heidi was learning English. The girls were best friends.

Heidi came over to play as we were finishing our breakfast. Susie washed her hands first and ran out; I was only a minute behind her. When I came out in the yard, the girls had vanished. I looked everywhere and could not find them. As I was about to leave, an acorn hit my head. Where did that come from? I was looking all over when another hit me, and another. What in the world? Then I heard Susie giggling. Where was she? I looked in the bushes, and another acorn hit me. Suddenly, I looked up in the tree and saw Susie and Heidi with a bag of acorns. They were throwing them at me. I shouted out, "How in the world did you get up in the tree?" The first limb towered at least ten feet off the ground with nowhere to climb, or so I thought. The girls started coming down, and what I saw next simply amazed me. They literally descended the last ten feet like monkeys embracing the tree.

After both girls were on the ground, Susie stated that Heidi could climb trees like a squirrel and had taught her. I immediately wished to learn this magic trick too! Heidi said something in German to Susie. Susie giggled, looked at me and responded in German. I nodded in agreement, to whatever my sister said. Heidi smiled big, grabbed my hand and pulled me to the tree. The tree climbing lessons began. She was very patient and helped me the rest of the morning. We never talked at all, mostly communicated with our hands and big smiles. My mom called me in for lunch and broke the spell. Heidi and I were having so much fun together. We stared at each other like neither wanted to go, as if we would never see each other again. I had such a strange feeling that didn't make sense to me. Heidi finally smiled, said "Auf Wiedersehen," and ran home.

I suddenly realized Susie had not been around while I played alone with Heidi. Where was she, and why didn't I miss her?

Susie was eating lunch when I came in. My first question was, "Where were you hiding all morning?" She replied, "Heidi already taught me to climb a tree, you needed private lessons.

"What! You could've stayed and translated." She answered, "You didn't need any help." Susie started singing, "Heidi and Pete, sitting in a tree, k-i-s-s-i-n-g..."

"What! We were not!" My sister ignored my protests and continued singing, "First comes love, then comes marriage, then comes Pete pushing a baby carriage..." I quickly realized that strange feeling with Heidi was love! How did Susie know?

I began to quiz Susie, "Do you think Heidi likes me?"

"Of course, she said she did right in front of you."

"What? Does she know I like her?" Susie giggled and said, "Of course, you told her you did."

"What?"

I realized Susie was not translating our desire to climb trees together; she recognized our desire for each other. My sister sensed a much deeper feeling between us. I finally admitted that Susie was right, and I did like Heidi very much. Susie smiled and said, "We'll always be first in each other's heart; but we can share our best friend."

Chapter 8 – The Man in the Moon

The entire world had stood still and watched Neil Armstrong and Buzz Aldrin walk on the moon the night before. This afternoon, all the kids were playing in the towering red, white, and blue space rocket. The entire park glistened in American colors after a fresh coat of paint for the Fourth of July festivities. The tall rocket appeared especially daunting and magnificent on this warm day in July. The other playground equipment stood unusually silent and ignored.

My sister and I had played on the big rocket many times at the park. Today, we respected this sculpture as if it were the Statue of Liberty. Susie wanted to climb to the top, fly to the moon, and shake hands with Neil and Buzz.

The boys laughed and said girls could not be astronauts. Susie asked why? The boys answered that only men could fly to the moon. That was all my sister needed to hear; she was about to prove them wrong.

Susie challenged the boys to jump out of the swing and fly like real astronauts. The three who landed the farthest would fly to the moon in the massive red, white, and blue space rocket and thank Neil and Buzz for being true Americans. My sister always went beyond her limits to win, and I worried she might hurt herself. What was I thinking? She's Susie! She never failed to prove a point! She was going to be the first girl astronaut commander of the space rocket. I wanted to be with my sister on the moon.

The boys swung as high as we dared and jumped. The three who went the farthest stood at the distance they landed. I ended up being second and upset. Either way, I was not going to walk on the moon with Susie. However, I knew we would be flying together.

Susie went last. She swung back and forth, going higher and higher, almost doing a loop-the-loop. Nobody ever swung that high! We were scared and afraid to watch.

Susie let go and soared over all of us like an American eagle. She landed skillfully, an Olympic score of an undisputed ten with both hands up high. The eagle has landed! My sister was going to be the first girl astronaut to shake the hands of Neil and Buzz on the moon!

The three of us walked back to the tall space rocket. Susie climbed to the top first as the commander, followed by the lunar module pilot, and I went last as the command module pilot. Everyone else stood back and watched. At the top,

Susie laid down in the middle with her crew on either side. I felt proud being next to my sister. She was flying me to the moon!

Susie asked, "Are all systems go for launch?" We both replied, "Roger." Susie shouted, "Mission Control, all systems are go, we're ready for lift-off." Suddenly everybody below started shouting, "Ten, nine, eight...." all the way down to zero. We heard everybody shout, "Liftoff!" We were excited! Then the massive rocket started shaking violently and we almost peed in our pants. A few kids were our big rocket engines in the bottom level. Everybody began yelling and clapping; we were going to the moon!

Commander Susie held her hands out steering us on our journey. Everything was quiet for a minute, and then she shouted, "Houston, the Eagle has landed."

Susie and her pilot stood up. The commander looked at me and said, "Wait for us, we'll be right back." They commenced climbing down the ladder as I got up and gazed at the slide far below. Everybody was doing the same.

Susie came down the slide first and stopped just short of putting her feet down. Then she firmly stomped in the sand, stood up, and loudly proclaimed, "That's one small step for a girl, one giant leap for everybody!"

Nobody said a word and we all watched intently, just like the night before on TV. I was proud of Susie and wanted to be on the surface with her. I shared the feelings with Michael Collins, knowing his friends were on the moon while he waited alone in Columbia.

Susie's colleague came down the slide next and they both walked in slow motion, kicking the sand on the moon. Susie stopped and shook hands with Neil Armstrong. Then turned and shook the hand of Buzz Aldrin. I rubbed my eyes! Neil and Buzz were in the park shaking hands with Susie! I told Michael Collins over the radio that I was thinking of him too.

After a minute, I heard the astronauts climbing back up the ladder and quickly got into my position. Susie's head popped up in the capsule and said, "NASA's so smart, why didn't they figure out how we could all walk on the moon together?" I knew my sister desired to walk with me too.

The commander and her lunar module pilot lay down in their positions. Susie gave the order, "Astronaut Pete, push the button and take us home. Shout 'Splashdown' when we land. That gesture of giving me authority as the pilot of the command module made me feel important. My sister was the best commander ever.

I grasped the steering wheel and drove to Earth for a minute, then shouted, "Splashdown!" as loud as I could. There was a huge cheer from the crowd below us. As we stood up, Susie said, "Pete, you go first, I'll slide down last" She planned to share the spotlight with her crew.

I slid down first to leave our rocket ship. All our friends began cheering for me. When Susie slid down, everybody went crazy cheering for the first girl on the moon! We waved at everybody, and they all shook our hands commending us on our mission. The crowd treated us like real heroes for a moment. I never played a game with so much emotion.

The sun was setting and the kids started leaving for home. A beautiful moon was rising. As I headed toward my bike, Susie knew I felt let down because we didn't walk on the moon together. Suddenly, there was a jerk on my hand as my sister pulled me back. Her eyes twinkled. "There's still time, let's be the first twins on the moon! You be the commander!"

A tear must have formed; Susie always said the perfect words to me. She gently wiped the tear away with a smile and said we needed to hurry.

As the commander, I welcomed my wonderful crew of one aboard our ship. We quickly climbed to the top, and I took the center position with Susie close by my side.

I asked in my best commander voice, "Are all systems go for launch?" Susie giggled, "Why do they say Roger? Your name is Peter." Only my sister would think of something funny like that; she made me laugh. I directed her to press the button and fly us to the moon again. She knew the way. Susie shouted "Liftoff," and we both started kicking the floor. The metal vibrated under us and my sister and I were on our voyage to the moon again.

The beautiful moon rose in the deep blue sky as the sun slowly set. We both silently stared at the sight in awe.

Suddenly, I realized we were going to be late for supper and get in trouble again. "Astronaut Susie, there's the moon. Hurry and land the rocket!" with a slightly panicked voice. Susie snapped out of the trance and she slammed both feet down hard with a loud boom that shook the space rocket.

"We've landed on the moon!"

Both of us quickly scampered down the ladder to the slide. Susie told me to go first, since I was the commander. On the way sliding down, I hadn't considered what to say as the first twins on the moon.

My feet hit the sand hard as I stood up, shouting my first thought. "I've got the best sister in the whole world!"

With that, my sister slid down with a big smile. She hugged me tight and said, "I've got the man in the moon."

Chapter 9 – Bully's Eye

Every class has a bully, and Mickey was ours. They intimidate the kids that they feel won't retaliate. Today, he threatened to beat me up on our walk home from school. Moreover, if Susie helped, he would beat her up too!

Just before we went outside to play kickball for recess, I informed Susie, "We can't walk home together. Mickey is going to beat me up, and I don't want you to get beat up too." My sister calmly said, "There's not a chance I won't walk home with you. That's all I look forward to every day. We need to teach him a lesson!" Susie never fails at anything. I knew we would be walking home together this afternoon.

Mickey always played kickball on the pitcher's mound to be at the center of attention, and nobody kicks the ball there anyway. I was playing at second base; Susie played on the opposing team that day. When Susie kicks, everybody backs way up—mostly for protection, because she always kicks the ball extremely hard. Only I knew that my sister was up to something and suddenly realized what her plan might be. A cold shiver ran down my spine. Susie was going to kill Mickey!

The ball sat squarely on home plate; Susie backed up and ran fast to kick the ball as she always does.

At the sound of her foot hitting the ball, all the fielders cringed, wondering if the ball would be coming at them like a speeding bullet. The ball was a low liner, very hard, and aimed right at Mickey on the pitcher's mound.

In a flash, the ball smacked Mickey square in the nose and bounced right back to home plate. Nobody saw what happened or where the ball went! All of a sudden, Mickey was flat on the ground, holding his nose, and crying like a baby. Everybody froze, not knowing what to do, except Susie. She skipped around the bases, smiling and waving while totally ignoring Mickey in pain on the field. My sister stopped on second base and stood there staring at Mickey before anybody knew what occurred or where the ball went. Mickey got up and ran back to the school building holding his bloody nose and crying. I finally regained my composure and walked over to see Susie. I told her, "I worried you were going to kill Mickey; thank goodness he's still alive." She smiled and said, "We can talk on our way home TOGETHER."

On our way home, I asked Susie if she thought Mickey would get even. I was nervous he might be mad at us now. She said, "Oh, I doubt it. He won't fight anybody that can actually beat him up. Plus, I stopped by the nurse's office to see how he was doing and apologized for making his nose bleed. He had a large ice pack on his face, but the nurse said nothing broke and he would be fine. I said goodbye and reminded him we were playing dodge ball tomorrow and hoped he would be back at school to be in the game." Then I heard her infectious giggle.

I threw my books on the ground and gave my sister a big hug!

Chapter 10 – Lost Her Marbles

The weather remained dreary the day after Thanksgiving. Susie and I played inside, trying to keep each other entertained. My sister decided she wanted to play a game of "keepsies" with me. While she played tennis exceptionally well, marbles was my game. We went to our rooms to fetch our marbles and met back in the living room for the big event. Susie did not have many marbles and played them all as I counted out mine to match hers. I only played ones that didn't mean much to me. She had never seen all the marbles I won playing other kids. Susie mixed them up thoroughly, and I laid the string around the marbles in a circle. My sister fired the first shot at the pile and the match commenced. I ended up winning the game with the most marbles. Losing the game did not bother Susie as much as losing her favorite cat's eye marbles to me. She was very disappointed.

At breakfast the next morning, Susie came into the warm kitchen and coolly sat down at her place at the large oak table. Still upset about losing her favorite marbles, she hardly touched her bowl of cereal, or the scrambled eggs and toast that Mom made for us. Mom even asked if anything was bothering her. My sister told her indifferently, "No, everything is just fine," as she finished and asked to be excused. Before getting out of her chair, I asked, "Did you look under your pillow this morning? The Marble Fairy replaces your favorite marbles, if you lose them to someone who loves you." Susie quickly leapt up and ran to check. Lo and behold, her favorite cat's eye marbles were in a little bag under her pillow. There was a loud shriek of glee from her room.

Susie happily returned with a confused expression on her face. How could this be? Was there really a Marble Fairy? She quizzed mom for an explanation. Mom did not have an answer for a question she did not even understand. Then Mom glanced at me and gently smiled.

The next month on Christmas Day, Mom passed out the gifts from under the tree to everyone. All of us were receiving the appropriate gift from Santa, and the yearly ritual went exactly as mom planned. There were even gifts from Russell that he sent from Vietnam that year. We were especially grateful to feel his essence celebrating the Christmas tradition, even though he was very far away. We especially missed his being with us.

Then a startled expression appeared on Mom's face as she came across a small gift that she did not recognize. She looked at me and said, "You seem to have received a gift from the Marble Fairy." Now I was confused, opening the gift. Lo and behold, there were a pair of cat's eye marbles in a small bag. Mom asked, "Who is this Marble Fairy in our house?" Susie instantly replied, almost shouting, "The Marble Fairy replaces your favorite marbles, if you lose them to someone who loves you." My sister understood the meaning of the Marble Fairy and we loved each other very much. There was nothing left to do, except place the bag on the sacred family knick-knack shelf in the living room.

Those cat's eye marbles were never played again and are still on the shelf to this day.

Chapter 11 – Tennis Is For the Birds

One day while walking in the park to play tennis, Susie and I noticed an elderly man feeding a million birds. The birds fascinated Susie, and she wanted to go see. This was the first instance I ever saw my sister distracted from playing tennis. We heard the man whistling like the birds. We slowly approached him where he was sitting on the bench; we did not want to scare them. He asked us to come over; the birds were his friends. Susie went right up and sat down next to him, her eyes staring in amazement. She asked, "Are you talking to the birds?" The man chuckled and said, "Of course, we talk every day." He gave my sister some birdseed and told her to lay it on the bench next to her. When she did, the birds ruffled and flew up beside her to eat the seed. That was the first occasion the man heard Susie's infectious giggle, and he laughed himself. He noticed her tennis racket and asked if she was any good. I said proudly, "She has a scorcher serve and even the high school kids ask to play. That gives me a break from chasing the balls all the time."

The man said he played tennis with his wife until she passed away several years ago. Now he feeds the birds in the park. He teased my sister, saying, "I'll wait until you grow up, then marry you to play tennis." Of course, he only said that to hear her infectious giggle.

We always visited our friend whenever we went to the park. He often stopped by the tennis court and cheered for Susie. Sometimes he even brought both of us ice cream.

One day, our friend was missing from the park. The birds were quiet. Then the days turned into weeks. Susie became nervous and worried. I reassured her, "He probably went on vacation and will be back soon."

Toward the end of summer, a nice lady saw us playing on the court. She came over, and asked Susie her name. My sister replied rather timidly, "Susie." The lady told us her father spoke of Susie often. Susie brought him great joy, and the lady desired to meet her father's tennis friend at the park. Susie trembled when asking, "Is he ok?" The lady smiled and said yes; he had a painful cancer and was finally comfortable in Heaven. Susie almost whispered, "Is he playing tennis with his wife?" A tear formed in the lady's eye, and she said, "He's running all over the court like Pete. My mother was a much better player than my father."

Susie started to sniffle, and the lady held her close. She said that she missed her father a great deal also. The lady gently sobbed. I had tears in my eyes; we were all sad. My sister eventually let go of the lady and looked tearfully at her face. The lady smiled back and said, "I'm glad my father made such a wonderful friend. He'll always be watching you from Heaven."

The lady gave Susie and myself one last hug, then turned and left. We watched her cross the park, get in her car, and drive away in silence. After she departed, we realized we never asked the man his name. Who was he? Susie's eyes were still moist. We had forgotten to ask the lady his name and we would never know.

When we got home, Mom obviously realized something troubling happened to Susie. We had spoken often of our friend at the park, and we told her that we found out he was comfortable in Heaven today. She took my sister to her room and let her take a nap. When Dad came home, Mom informed him on what had occurred and they let her sleep through supper.

Later that night, we decided to name our friend "Admiral Bird" and added him in our prayers. Susie wanted to be sure he would take a break from playing tennis with his wife and watch her sometime.

Chapter 12 – Jingle Bell Tag

Susie wore her jingle bells for the Christmas season and said to me, "Let's go see if Danny can come out to play freeze tag." My sister and I never went to his house before. Danny was a cute boy and very friendly. He was also blind. We knocked on the door and Danny's mother answered. Susie asked, "Can Danny come out to play? We know he doesn't come out often. We'll be extra careful and make sure nothing happens to him except have fun." How could any mother refuse Susie? She had a reputation of being incredibly trustworthy. His mom invited us inside and said, "Why don't you ask him." She called out to Danny that he had company.

Danny arrived in the living room, and before his mother could tell him anything, Susie exclaimed, "Hi, Danny!" He obviously recognized her voice. A huge smile formed and he eagerly replied, "Susie!" My sister asked Danny if he would like to come out and play freeze tag. With a puzzled look he questioned, "How am I able to play?"

Susie walked toward him as her bells jingled with every step. Danny followed her motion precisely while constantly moving to face her. Susie told him, "You obviously know where I am." Then she reached out giggling and touched him, "Freeze! All you have to do is keep away from me!" Danny sparkled when he felt my sister's hand; he certainly did not want to keep away from her.

His mom asked us if we would make sure he doesn't go into the street. I told her, "Going in the street is cheating, and Susie yells at anybody who tries. Plus all the kids will watch and keep him safe." My sister informed his mom that we play in our yard in the next block, and that she would hold his hand to guide him. His mom laughed and advised Danny, "It's up to you, but you better not turn down holding a pretty girl's hand." I chimed in, "The other boys are going to be jealous." Danny said with a big smile, "Let's go!"

When we got to our house, Susie instructed the other kids, "I'll be 'It' and Danny is going to try and keep away from my jingle bells. Everybody call out for Danny when you're frozen, so he knows where you are."

The game began and Susie ran near Danny without tagging him while he became used to the sound of her bells. As she tagged other kids, they called out for Danny to unfreeze them. Danny was getting good, and Susie finally touched him. He had a huge smile while standing frozen. We continued to play until dusk when parents started calling the kids home.

Susie told everybody, "Bring bells tomorrow so Danny can be 'It' and chase everybody wearing bells." With that, the last of the kids left to go home. Susie walked over to Danny and asked, "Are you ready to go home?" He replied, "Are you kidding, let's play some more!" My sister and I looked at each other; neither of us knew how to answer. He finally laughed, knowing he pulled a good joke on us. We never thought of that; he could play in the dark.

Then he asked Susie, "Can I follow your jingle bells home? I'm really used to the sound now and know exactly where you are!" Susie had a panicked look. That was not what she wanted to hear. I saw my sister's face and told Danny, "You should hold Susie's hand, especially when crossing the street. Cars can't see you at night." It became obvious that I did not need to say anything when I noticed his big smile. He pulled another good joke on us.

Danny asked her, "Will you hold my hand and walk me home?" Susie said with a gentle voice, "Of course, that was the offer from a pretty girl." She said to me, "Tell Mom I'm walking Danny home."

I saw my sister growing up and walking away holding the hand of the boy she truly liked. How long would it take Danny to figure Susie out? Knowing Susie, probably the rest of his life.

Chapter 13 – Horse of a Different Color

Dad put up a makeshift basketball goal for us along the driveway, using an old piece of plywood for the backboard. At least Susie and I did not need to ride our bikes to the park to practice shooting baskets. It was a nice spring afternoon and we were playing a game of Horse. Susie decided to shoot an outrageous long shot on "S" for Susie. I just shook my head when she missed and watched the ball bounce over the fence into the neighbor's yard. The neighbors didn't have any children except for a large boxer dog named Pee Wee. When the ball went over the fence, we always asked the neighbors if they would get the ball for us. They were very nice and always did. The couple took us into the backyard and told Pee Wee, "Susie and Pete are here to get the ball," as Pee Wee sat and watched. She never growled, although we never asked to pet her either. We obviously treated her with great respect and never went into the yard without the neighbors. Honestly, we were both afraid of big Pee Wee.

Susie and I went next door to ask the neighbors if they could get our basketball. Today nobody answered after we rang the doorbell several times. The neighbors were gone. We hadn't seen or heard Pee Wee in the backyard and assumed the neighbors took her with them. My sister decided she would go into the backyard and get the basketball while I guarded the gate and held it open.

As Susie picked up the ball and started to walk out, we heard a loud bark. Pee Wee had been sleeping in the backyard! Susie threw the ball over the fence and bolted toward the open gate. I saw Pee Wee chasing after her and could not decide, would we get into more trouble if Pee Wee got out or if she ate Susie for a snack. My sister was shrieking and running for her life. I noticed Pee Wee galloping behind wanting to play. She could easily overtake Susie. I decided to leave the gate open and let Susie through. As she went screaming past me, Pee Wee came to a stop, placed her head against my hand, and gave me a loving lick. The neighbors trained Pee Wee! That was why they introduced us when we were in the backyard. She knew we were friends.

I fondly rubbed Pee Wee behind the ears and told her she was a good girl, then closed the gate and petted her one last time as I left to search for Susie. I found my sister sitting on the front porch, still scared after Pee Wee almost ate her. When she saw me, she asked, "How are we going to get Pee Wee back in the yard?" I calmed my sister and said, "Pee Wee never left and would never hurt us. She was a trained guard dog and knew we were her friends."

The next day, Susie and I spotted the neighbor's car in the driveway and went to tell them what happened. We described how the ball accidently went over the fence and promised never to go in the yard again without their permission. However, we asked if we could play with Pee Wee when my sister and I asked their approval.

The couple laughed and invited us inside, explaining that they visited the doctor's office yesterday and were having a baby. We became the first to know! The neighbors appreciated we came over and asked to play with Pee Wee; she needed to start being around children now. We were welcome in the backyard anytime. They declared that since we acted so respectful and honest, they knew where to find dependable babysitters.

Chapter 14 - Down There by the Train

A few small, steep hills made good jumps to ride bicycles near the train trestle. Susie was afraid to ride her bike over the jumps, although she sometimes came and watched the boys be daredevils. The boys formed a secret trestle club, mainly because girls were never around. To join, you sat under the nearby low bridge while a train went over. I was a member and sat under the trestle several times. However, not a single person ever kept sitting under the trestle with a train traveling fast overhead on their first time. We were careful and knew nobody would get hurt, yet the loud noise of the train right over your head was terrifying!

Susie happened to be there when we heard the loud whistle of the approaching train. I asked my sister if she wanted to join the club; she would be the first girl. Of course, she ran under the bridge with me. We could hear the train coming as the clickety-clack got louder and louder.

The train horn blew, and the acceptance ritual began. The train clamored only a few feet right over our heads—a million tons of fast moving steel. A couple of the boys immediately ran out. The noise of the train vibrating loudly under the small trestle grew deafening. Susie grabbed onto my arm and yelled at me, "Pete, I'm scared!" She was not letting go. I yelled back, "Don't be scared, you're safe with me. There's nothing to be afraid of." A minute went by and another boy ran out. My sister held on to me for dear life. I could not breathe! She was too frightened to run!

Finally, the train passed and everything became quiet. There were three boys and Susie left under the trestle. All three of us had been underneath the train before and knew what to expect, but Susie remained terrified. I calmed her down and we walked out into the sunlight. Some of the boys started laughing at my sister, and I demanded they stop. Not only was she the first girl to join the club, she got in on the first try! Nobody ever did that before. We then got on our bikes and quietly rode home.

I told Mom that a dog chased Susie, and she wasn't feeling good. My sister did look rather tired and pale. Mom excused her from dinner to lie down and rest; she could have a snack later when she woke up.

The next day Susie walked silently to school, afraid that everybody was going to tease her for being scared. However, everybody appeared excited when we reached the school. They all praised Susie on becoming the first girl in the trestle club, and she joined on the first try. She was the newest member. Moreover, she gave confidence to other girls and boys to join the trestle club. Many kids were afraid to sit under the track with a million tons of steel speeding loudly down the track overhead.

We all learned it was wise to be fearful of the unknown and find assurance in ourselves when seeing others overcome their fears.

Chapter 15 – Leap Toad

Susie and I were always partners playing games, and today the kids decided to play leapfrog. Except my sister asked Danny to be her partner, since he never played this game before in his life. I was slightly miffed at her for not picking me; however, I realized Danny trusted Susie the most. He became competitive playing games with us, and the kids often forgot he was blind. My sister and I both liked Danny very much. Danny told her, "All the boys say you look like a toad, but I trust Pete telling me you're beautiful." Susie giggled and replied, "I'll call the game 'leap toad' just for you." Since for the first time my sister and I were not partners Heidi came up and asked me, "Will you be my partner?" I suddenly found a frog in my throat and could not utter a simple, "Yes, I'd love to be your partner." Finally, I nodded my head up and down to accept her offer, like a toad.

Susie and Danny were going to compete against us in the first race across the lawn. We started, and the kids began cheering. The noise confused Danny's bearings and he drifted wildly off course. Susie tried pointing him back to the finish line. It was obvious that Danny became discouraged, not knowing what to do. I appreciated he did not want to let Susie down. That is a feeling I often have also. By now, we were far ahead of them and at the finish line. All Heidi had to do was leap over me to win.

However, Heidi sat on my back and shouted at Danny to come toward her. She tried to disguise her voice so he would not recognize who was attempting to help him, just as Susie would. I grew confused with who sat on my back. Heidi or Susie? Hearing Heidi's voice let Danny pinpoint his position. Danny and Susie started going in the right direction and caught up to us. Heidi continued to yell until Danny was next to me. Susie had a big smile when she leaped over his back and they won. Heidi then jumped over mine to conclude the race. Danny won his first game of leapfrog!

He appeared very excited and gave Susie a big hug. Oh my, what was happening? Heidi became Susie and let Danny win. I suddenly gave Heidi a big hug, like my sister, and told her, "You're the best." Heidi giggled and held me like Susie. Where was I? Win or lose, I felt very happy.

We sat down together to watch the next race. Girls with girls, boys with boys. Danny thanked me for letting him win, which I confessed that Heidi actually did. She took charge, just like Susie. He laughed and understood exactly what I meant. He divulged that he felt special because everybody encouraged him to play games like a sighted person. He realized they were behind and being lost frustrated him. He then said, "I always feel safe and enjoy when Susie is near me." She tried to guide him, but Heidi could never hide her German accent and he honed right in on her voice. I divulged to him, "I always feel safe and enjoy when Heidi is near me too."

We both laughed that the girls were taking control of our lives, and we were not even trying to stop them. I warned him, "We need to be careful with those two girls, they're definitely not toads."

Chapter 16 – Lava

Our parents went to see a movie one summer evening and trusted us to stay home and not get into trouble. Soon as they left, Susie wanted to play lava. The game is to jump from one piece of furniture to another without falling into the molten lava on the floor. The rule is to scream if you fall in. Susie was good and never lost. I always fell in, having fun flailing around on the floor and screaming. My sister enjoyed the extra drama and often applauded after my performance. I appreciated her recognition and never wasted the chance to play with Susie.

We moved the furniture around in the living room and made an obstacle course. I jumped and fell in a few times. Now I began chiding Susie to take more chances. She indulged my badgering and sprang from the chair, across the coffee table, and landed on the sofa. She suddenly tumbled on the cushions and screamed in pain. Why was this? My sister didn't need to scream; she landed safely on the couch. She shrieked again and at once grabbed her ankle. Then I realized Susie had twisted her ankle between the cushions when she lost her balance and fell. I calmed her down, ran to find a towel, and filled it with ice from the freezer. Susie's ankle really swelled up!

What were we going to tell Mom and Dad when they came home from the movies? We were supposed to be asleep. Susie decided she could make it through the night with the ice pack on her ankle. That gave me until tomorrow to figure out a story to explain her sprain.

The next morning, Susie's ankle was still sore. As we were taking our places at the breakfast table, Dad asked what my sister and I did last night. We both stammered and said we just played. Then Mom came to the table and looked at us. She asked, "What did you do last night? There's no ice in the freezer and all the trays are empty."

Uh-oh. In all the excitement moving the furniture back by myself, I forgot to refill the ice trays.

I confessed, "We were playing marbles, and I wanted to jump on the sofa. Susie said no, that's dangerous. I jumped anyway and tumbled, the fall scared me. Susie ran to bring me a glass of water and twisted her ankle when she accidently slipped on the marbles. Susie suffered all night because she didn't want me to get into trouble."

Dad glared at me and sternly said, "Young man, you're grounded to your room for three days. You can only come out to eat meals with the family and go to the bathroom. You will remain in your room without seeing any friends. Is this understood?"

Looking down at the floor, I quietly said, "Yes, sir."

Susie suddenly blurted out, "Pete always protects me. He didn't do anything wrong. I was the one jumping on the couch and twisted my ankle between the cushions. He only wrapped the ice in a towel and put it on my ankle to reduce the pain. He helped me into bed, and then he sat with me until I finally fell asleep."

Mom looked at Dad, not knowing what to say. Dad turned away from me and faced Susie. My sister was also looking down at the floor. She tried to tell the truth and protect me from punishment. We were both in big trouble now! Our dad asked her if she needed to see the doctor, and said he would take her. She gently shook her head and softly said, "No, sir."

Next Dad sternly said to her, ""Young lady, you're grounded to Russell's room for three days. You will sleep in Russell's bed and only come out to eat meals with the family or go to the bathroom. You may only go into your own room to change clothes. You will remain in Russell's room without seeing any friends. Is this understood?" She faintly said, "Yes, sir."

I felt very confused. Susie and I were being punished by not seeing our friends or go outside to play during summer vacation. Isolated from the world together in the same room did not amount to any punishment at all! However, I then realized we would not survive being isolated from each other for three days! I decided not to ask for clarification and determine if we could play together in my room.

I am certain my dad knew the consequence when he made the decision to ground us together. He understood that our bond became inseparable as my sister and I dealt with the unknown of our brother in Vietnam. My parents grew deeply attached to each other for the same reason.

Chapter 17 – Bad Mitten

Susie competed in all the racquet sports with natural ability and later became a star tennis player in college. She could beat me every time without trying and was always testing different ways to hit the ball. I usually ended up chasing all her serves, since they were so hard and fast, I could barely see them. Except for the ones that hit me. I couldn't get out of the way quickly enough.

Susie wanted to play badminton on a blustery cold January morning. We bundled up nice and warm, and went to the garage to locate the equipment. Everything was there but the birds. We searched all over the place for them. The tube of birds was missing. Where were the birds? This minor issue didn't deter Susie. She was eager to play and sacrificed one of her own mittens as a substitute. My sister and I quickly set up the net in the front yard. Susie prepared to decimate me.

We started the game, and of course, Susie ruthlessly scored the first points against me. After several minutes of playing in the icy weather without a mitten, her hand became cold and began to hurt as she hit the heavier mitten. My sister missed numerous volleys in a row, and I took the lead. By now, her hand visibly disturbed her and my face became frozen. I was thankful she did not smack me there with the mitten of ice.

I offered to go back inside where it was warm. Susie would hear nothing of quitting a game while losing. That would let me win by default, so the badminton match continued for several more minutes in the bitter cold. I noticed tears in her eyes from the pain my sister felt in her uncovered hand. I immediately called a time-out and ran over to her. I took my sister's frozen hand into mine and blew my breath to heat hers. After a short while, the numbness and tears of pain were gone. I gave her one of my gloves to wear for the rest of the game. My coat pocket kept my hand comfortable and did not cause much of a disadvantage. She was going to kick my rear end anyway.

Susie was happy, and the match continued. She made some impressive moves, which I always enjoy watching her make. Except she knocked that mitten solidly out of play every chance. Suddenly I won the match and the game ended! We both felt very cold and quickly went inside to our wonderfully warm home. Mom knew we were outside in the cold weather, and hot chocolate sat on the kitchen table waiting for us when we came in.

Susie and I enjoyed our cups of cocoa together by the fireplace. She thanked me for taking good care of her, saying that she possessed the best twin brother in the world. I declared that was my job; I could not be happy without the best twin sister in the world. We finished our drinks and decided to play inside the rest of that chilly day.

I'm certain she struck that bad mitten hard on purpose to finish the game. Susie takes good care of me too.

Chapter 18 – Lucy, I'm Home!

No kids were outside playing on this overcast and rainy day. Susie wanted to play house since we were inside. We acted the respective roles as the parents of our imaginary family. Today we had four children. Our household became as large as sixteen children when Susie used all her dolls. Susie knew how to have children. My sister would be good and quickly do everything Mom told her, then ask Mom for a new doll as a reward. Our dynasty grew.

Whenever Susie wanted to play with "our children" by herself, she sent me out of the room and ordered, "Go to work now." I did not have any idea what I was supposed to do and frequently sat on the living room couch until she told me to come home. Sometimes she made me wait an hour before summoning me back.

I decided to go over and play with Danny and left the house without telling Susie. Susie decided to call me home early from work today! She was furious at not finding me. My sister finally discovered me at Danny's house after searching everywhere in the neighborhood along the way. That's when the big trouble started. Susie stormed into Danny's room, then yelled at me very loudly that I was playing with her first and under no condition should have left without telling her.

She became a demon possessed! I never saw her this angry playing a game.

Susie firmly grabbed my ear with a painful twist and made me follow her back home. Danny stood petrified at the sound of Susie and thankful he was not at the focus of her attention this time. Danny's mother could barely control her laughter; she knew Susie was giving both Danny and me a lesson we would never forget. She loved Susie like her own daughter.

When my sister and I finally arrived home, my ear was bright red from her solid grip. Susie demanded that I sleep on the couch. She forbade me to leave our home until she finished playing house. After almost an hour, she called me into her room with a stern voice. My sister gave me a lecture on never leaving the house without telling her where she could find me. She expected me to be nearby, or at least expected to know where to look in an emergency. She asked, "What would happen if one of our children became sick and needed your help?" I could only look at the ground silently, since I didn't have an answer. She asked again in a louder voice, "Well?" I remained quiet as I shifted back and forth uneasily. Susie continued, "I may not have time to find you!"

I never thought about that. Now I understood why Dad always told Mom his destination whenever he left home. He called her when departing work, even to run an errand at lunch. She knew where he was at all times. What if something happened to Susie or myself? Mom would need to inform him right away. What if there was an emergency and our parents had to find us? I began to appreciate why our parents always required knowing where we were going and how to reach us.

As a grown man, I make sure my wife knows where I am at all times. Danny does the same. We both have Susie to thank for that!

Chapter 19 – First Kiss

Our parents gave Susie and me a great birthday party and allowed us to invite all our classmates from school. We played different games in the yard for over an hour, and then took a break to have punch and birthday cake. Susie enjoyed her favorite, devil's food cake, and I ate my angel food. Everybody had a big slice. After we finished opening presents, Mom announced that the birthday girl could pick the next game to play. I grumbled that I came into the world a full five minutes earlier than she did. She reminded me that ladies are always first before gentlemen. With that, Mom asked Susie what game she wanted to play.

My sister loudly exclaimed, "Spin the bottle!"

That was the last game Mom expected and caught her by complete surprise. As I remember this moment, we were experiencing our first feelings of adulthood and the days of cooties were fading away. All the kids squealed with excitement. I knew Susie liked Danny and she was looking for any excuse to kiss him. Mom looked at the other parents while shrugging her shoulders, not knowing if this was appropriate and wanting approval from anybody. With the kids pleading to play, all the parents nodded. Let the game begin.

Dad stood up to take control and directed all the kids to sit in a circle, boy then girl. Next, he sat Susie directly across from me. He held up a 12-ounce bottle of Coca-Cola, regally popped the bottle cap off, and drank the entire bottle in one gulp. He raised his arms to the heavens, and released the biggest, loudest burp ever heard by humans. Everybody laughed so hard our sides hurt. Mom shielded her face with her hands, shaking her head and looking down at the floor. Who was this strange man in our living room?

Dad asked everybody that kissed before to raise their hand. Nobody moved a muscle.

Dad placed the bottle on the ground in the middle of the group, and then asked Susie to come forward and kneel beside the empty bottle. Susie went first. My dad told everyone that this was a special moment. "Remember your first kiss and carry that precious memory the rest of your life."

This ended the ceremony and Susie placed her hand tepidly on the bottle. She gazed at every boy around the circle to see who her first kiss might be, with a secret peek at Danny. Every boy in that room prayed the bottle would point at them. The drama grew intense. Her birthday wish might not come true. She gave the bottle a good spin and hoped for the best. The bottle spun around three complete times, then slowed down to point at the lucky boy.

The bottle finally stopped and pointed directly at me!

How could Susie fail at anything and cause this to happen! How could I be the lucky boy! Everybody was laughing and whooping it up. This bizarre coincidence on the first spin even amused the parents. I immediately protested, but all the kids teased and were insistent that I was a boy and those were the rules. My sister and I were the only brother and sister at the party, and everybody wanted to see us kiss. I reluctantly moved to the middle and joined Susie. I turned my head and pointed reassuringly at my cheek. This would not turn into another drama moment. Susie leaned forward and started to kiss me.

Before she got there, I suddenly spun my face directly toward hers and we kissed square on the lips. My sister jumped back like a scared cat; all the kids started laughing and yelling in approval. No one ever saw that trick before. My sister had a look on her face somewhere between irritation and failure. This was not her birthday wish.

I whispered in her ear, "Russell told me about the trick before leaving. The kiss is from both of us."

Susie's expression changed as she looked at me tenderly and began to tear up. She leaned in and kissed me gently as only a loving sister could. "That's my first real kiss with a boy; always remember your first kiss."

Chapter 20 – Suppertime!

I began to reminisce and said, "Do you remember the time..."

Before another word came out, she gently said, "Of course, Pete. I always remember the time spent with you."

I asked Susie, "Know what I've been thinking about?" Of course she did.

"The games we played and the lessons we learned while Russell served in Vietnam. I wish he could be here this Christmas."

My sister and I both knew why our older brother could not be with us. His wife was also a fraternal twin and needed to be with her brother on special occasions. They were as close as Susie and I. And she's as pretty as Susie; our older brother is a lucky man. In addition, Russell is certainly enjoying the holiday with his old Vietnam War buddy, Jack. We'll see them next year. Only destiny could arrange a marriage from such improbable odds as meeting in a mess hall, or so I always thought.

I continued, "There's only one thing I never knew." She answered before I asked.

"You."

"What? I know you kissed me, but..."

"You! Dad said to always remember your first kiss and carry that precious memory the rest of your life. I wanted you as my precious memory."

"What?"

"Plus I saw you practicing Russell's silly trick in the mirror. You weren't going to waste that on Heidi at the party. She deserved better from you."

"What? How?"

"Susie, do you need help with the dishes?" came a soft voice from the living room with a slight German accent.

Susie replied, "No, Heidi, you enjoy watching the children. Pete and I are reminiscing while finishing up."

My sister continued, "I did pretty good on that one for you."

"I always thought you wanted to kiss Danny first."

A man's deep voice beckoned from the living room this time. "Hey, are you two reminiscing about that first kiss? Those chances were astronomical that the bottle would point at me. Susie was my first kiss! My toad became my princess!"

Danny never called Susie a toad since that day. Danny's vision of Susie was more beautiful than any man with sight could ever see.

Then Heidi reminded me, "And Pete was my first kiss on that magical day, too!"

Heidi continued, "Although there was nothing miraculous about us sharing this childhood story of our first kiss. I taught Susie how to climb a tree, she taught me how to spin the bottle and point at you!"

Every living creature in the house except Susie and Heidi shrieked after that bombshell, "WHAT!"

The coincidence of us all sharing the first kiss was completely Susie's making? Susie rigged the game? Did my sister control our destinies from childhood?

What am I thinking? Of course she did, she's Susie!

I never would have survived my childhood without my twin sister. What a wonderful life we share!

Then I heard Susie's infectious giggle.